Marvin Mammoth

16

Written by Jill Eggleton
Illustrated by Jim Storey

Rigby

Marvin looked after the park.
One morning he saw
a woolly mammoth
under the trees.
He stopped and stared.
"A woolly mammoth?"
he said to himself.
"I can't have a woolly
mammoth in this park!"

Marvin went to the library
to find out about
woolly mammoths.
He read . . .

Woolly Mammoths
Woolly mammoths
were like elephants.
They had long, woolly hair.
They had long tusks.
They lived in the ice
and snow.

8

"Woolly mammoths liked
cold places," said Marvin.
"I'll have to make
an ice cave.
Then I can catch
that woolly mammoth."

So Marvin made an ice cave
in the back of his truck.
He put the truck in the park.
Then he went home to wait
for the woolly mammoth
to go into the truck.

The next day,
Marvin went to the park.
He heard noises
in the ice truck.
"Good," said Marvin.
"That woolly mammoth
is in the truck.
I will take it back
to the ice and snow."

But when he looked inside,
the ice truck was full of . . .

"Seals!" said Marvin.
"This ice truck is not for seals.
It is for the woolly mammoth."
But the woolly mammoth was
nowhere to be seen.

Marvin put the ice truck
in the park every day.

He got penguins.
He got sea lions.
And he even got polar bears!

"Polar bears!"
said Marvin's friends.
"You can't put that ice truck
in the park anymore!"

Marvin still looks after
the park.
And sometimes
he sees big footprints
on the grass under the trees.
"That woolly mammoth
has been here again,"
he says.

Instructions

How to Make a Woolly Mammoth

You will need:

- newspaper
- old stocking
- colored card
- yarn or cotton
- glue or tape

1) Crumble up the newspaper. Put the paper in the stocking to make a body.

2) Tie the stocking at the end. Cut off the piece of stocking at the end.

3) Cut the yarn or cotton into long pieces to cover the body. Glue the yarn or cotton on.

4) Use the colored card to cut out:
eyes	tusks
trunk	tail

   Glue on to the woolly mammoth.

Guide Notes

Title: Marvin's Woolly Mammoth
Stage: Early (4) – Green

Genre: Fiction
Approach: Guided Reading
Processes: Thinking Critically, Exploring Language, Processing Information
Written and Visual Focus: Instructions
Word Count: 265

THINKING CRITICALLY
(sample questions)
- What do you think this story could be about?
- Look at pages 2 and 3. Who do you think this person could be? What do you know about woolly mammoths?
- Look at pages 4 and 5. Why do you think Marvin is putting ice into a truck?
- Look at pages 12 and 13. How do you think Marvin feels about the animals being in his swimming pool?

EXPLORING LANGUAGE

Terminology
Title, cover, illustrations, author, illustrator, title page

Vocabulary
Interest words: mammoth, tusks
High-frequency words: catch, heard
Compound words: himself, inside, nowhere, sometimes, footprints, newspaper, cardboard
Positional words: under, in, into, inside

Print Conventions
Capital letter for sentence beginnings, titles and names (**M**arvin), periods, quotation marks, commas, question mark, ellipses, exclamation marks